Shannon and the World's Tallest Leprechaun

Sean Callahan   Illustrated by **Kathleen Kemly**

Albert Whitman & Company, Morton Grove, Illinois

For Sophie and Charlotte, my favorite Irish dancers. —s.c.

For my mom—Bob. —k.k.

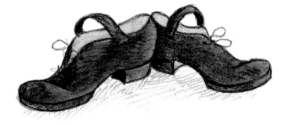

Library of Congress Cataloging-in-Publication Data

Callahan, Sean, 1965-
Shannon and the world's tallest leprechaun / by Sean Callahan ; illustrated by Kathleen Kemly.
p. cm.
Summary: Shannon has been practicing for the local St. Patrick's Day stepdancing competition,
but worries about her homemade dress and second-hand shoes until she summons
a very unusual leprechaun, hoping that he can help her do well.
ISBN 978-0-8075-7326-6 (hardcover)
[1. Leprechauns—Fiction. 2. Stepdancing—Fiction. 3. Dancing—Fiction. 4. Contests—Fiction.
5. Saint Patrick's Day—Fiction.] I. Kemly, Kathleen Hadam, ill. II. Title.
PZ7.C12974Sha 2008 [E]—dc22 2007030758

For more information about Albert Whitman & Company,
please visit our web site at www.albertwhitman.com.

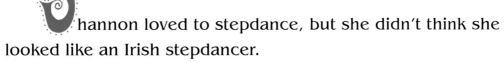

S hannon loved to stepdance, but she didn't think she looked like an Irish stepdancer.

Other girls had fancy wigs; she curled her own hair for competitions. Other girls had expensive dresses from Ireland; Shannon's mom had made her dress.

And other girls had brand-new hard shoes. Shannon had an old second-hand pair with scuffs no amount of shining could cover.

It was three days before the Saint Patrick's Day stepdance contest, held at the Irish-American Heritage Center. Shannon didn't think she'd win, but she was practicing anyway, when—with a loud, sharp crack—the heel snapped off her left shoe.

Oh, no! She knew her mom and dad couldn't afford to buy her new shoes. But how could she enter the contest with a broken heel?

It was hopeless. Blinking back tears, Shannon went outside to throw her shoes in the garbage. Suddenly she remembered something her dad had told her once when she was sad. If you closed your eyes and counted backward in Gaelic, the ancient Irish language, a leprechaun might appear to grant a wish.

There was nothing to lose. Shannon closed her eyes and counted, *"A hocht, a seacht, a se, a cuig, a ceathair, a tri, a do, a haon."*

She opened her eyes.

Standing before her was a bearded man wearing a shoemaker's leather apron. He looked just like she imagined a leprechaun would, except that he wasn't a wee man. "You must be six feet tall!" she blurted.

"If you must know," the man said, frowning, "I'm five-foot-eleven. I am Liam, the world's tallest leprechaun."

"Are you *really* a leprechaun?" Shannon asked.

"Yes, yes, yes!" Liam said, exasperated. "I get that all the time: 'Are you *sure* you're a leprechaun? You're way too *big* to be a leprechaun.' But let's get down to business. Because your counting has summoned me here, I'm obligated to grant you three wishes—one each day for the next three days."

Shannon thought only a moment. "I wish for a brand-new stepdance outfit: a wig, a beautiful dress, and shoes with heels that don't break off."

"A wig? A dress?" the leprechaun scoffed. "What do those have to do with dancing? But a shoe—you do need that. Give me your broken one. I'll show you how to take care of the perfectly fine stuff you already have."

He took the shoe, pulled a hammer and nails from his apron, and drove a nail through the heel and into the sole.

"Now you try," he said. Shannon pounded in another nail.

"Good as new, even better," the leprechaun said. "That's your first wish."

Before Shannon could protest that having her shoe repaired wasn't her wish at all, Liam had vanished.

At dinner, Shannon was very quiet. Her mother asked her what was wrong. "What do leprechauns look like?" Shannon asked.

Her dad laughed. "Well," he said, "they're usually drawn with beards."

"They're also pretty small," her mom added. "Maybe a foot high."

So how could that tall person be a leprechaun? Shannon wondered.

After school the next day, Shannon rushed to the backyard. Would the leprechaun return? She was about to count backwards in Gaelic when there he was, wagging his finger in her face.

"No need to count again," he said grumpily. "I'm a leprechaun who does what he says he'll do. Let's have that second wish, lass."

Shannon was ready. "I wish I were a great Irish stepdancer," she said.

"Did you know the best way to get better at something is to teach someone else how to do it?" demanded Liam. "This afternoon you'll be showing *me* how to dance."

Now Shannon was grumpy. "Don't you ever just grant wishes? Does everyone have to work so hard?"

"I'm no fairy godmother," Liam said. "I grant wishes in a proper manner."

"Are you really a leprechaun? You sure don't look like one."

Liam glowered at her. "I know I'm very tall," he said. "But I'm the best leprechaun that ever was. How I *look* doesn't matter. How I grant wishes does. Now, show me how to dance!"

So on the patio, in the cool March air,
Shannon started the leprechaun's dance lesson.
She showed him how to hold his arms at his sides
and keep his head high and his back straight.
Then she demonstrated a simple treble jig. "Floor,
knee, hop back, two, three, four," she called.

At first Liam danced like a rag doll, his limbs going every which way. But after a long, grueling practice, they were dancing together in perfect time.

"You know, I think that's the best I've ever danced," Shannon said, out of breath.

"What did I tell you about teaching, lass?" the leprechaun said. "It's great practice."

Shannon closed her eyes and wiped some sweat from her face. When she opened her eyes again, Liam was gone.

Shannon ran into the house. "If you met a leprechaun, what would you wish for?" she asked her dad.

"Gold, of course," her father said. "Leprechauns are supposed to hide a pot of gold at the end of the rainbow. Why all the questions about leprechauns?"

"Oh . . . you know, Saint Patrick's Day and all," Shannon said at last.

The next day Liam again appeared in the backyard. Right away Shannon asked, "Do you have a pot of gold buried at the end of the rainbow?"

"Aye, it's true," Liam said. "Did you Google me or something?"

"Is it within the rules for me to wish for some of your gold?"

"'Tis, and if you practice some more, tomorrow on Saint Patrick's Day you will have some," he said, grinning.

Again, the leprechaun and Shannon danced together. When Liam disappeared, for the first time ever Shannon felt she could win.

It was drizzling on Saint Patrick's Day as Shannon walked confidently to the Irish-American Heritage Center. But when she saw Bridget in her fine curly wig, Colleen in her fancy dress, and Meg in her new hard shoes, Shannon began to lose heart. She just didn't *look* like a stepdancer.

It was her turn to dance. She went onstage with only her own curls, wearing her homemade dress and scuffed-up hard shoes. Now it was raining even harder. Oh, what was the point?

She looked out at the crowd. There were her mom and dad, smiling at her. She gave them a little smile back. Then she saw the leprechaun! His silly hat towered over the crowd, and he winked at her.

Shannon took a deep breath. If Liam could grant wishes looking nothing like a leprechaun, maybe she could dance in her old shoes!

When the violinist started to play, Shannon thought only about dancing. Her curls bounced, her dress swirled, and her shoes thumped. She danced the most beautiful treble jig she had ever danced.

Treble Jig Score
Meghan 3 4 3 10
Shannon 5 5
Mary
Katie

The rain stopped, and the sun broke through the clouds. Shannon curtsied and the crowd cheered. Someone shouted, "Brilliant!" She knew it was Liam.

When Shannon won first prize, she caught sight of a rainbow arcing across the sky. It seemed to point right to the shining medal hanging around her neck. So this was the leprechaun's gold!

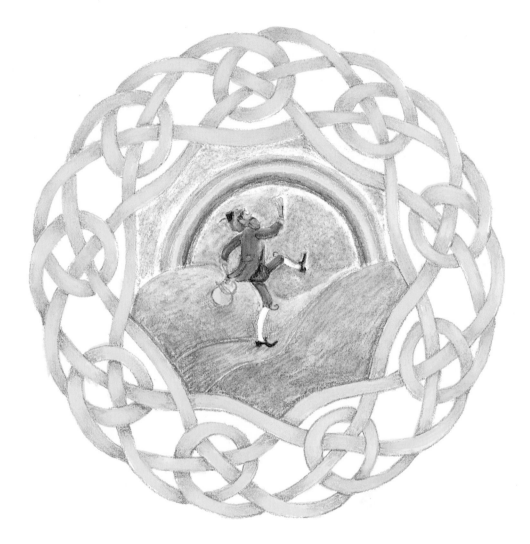

She looked for Liam in the crowd; he had vanished once more. But she could have sworn she heard him whisper in her ear, "Happy Saint Patrick's Day, Shannon!"